W9-ART-811

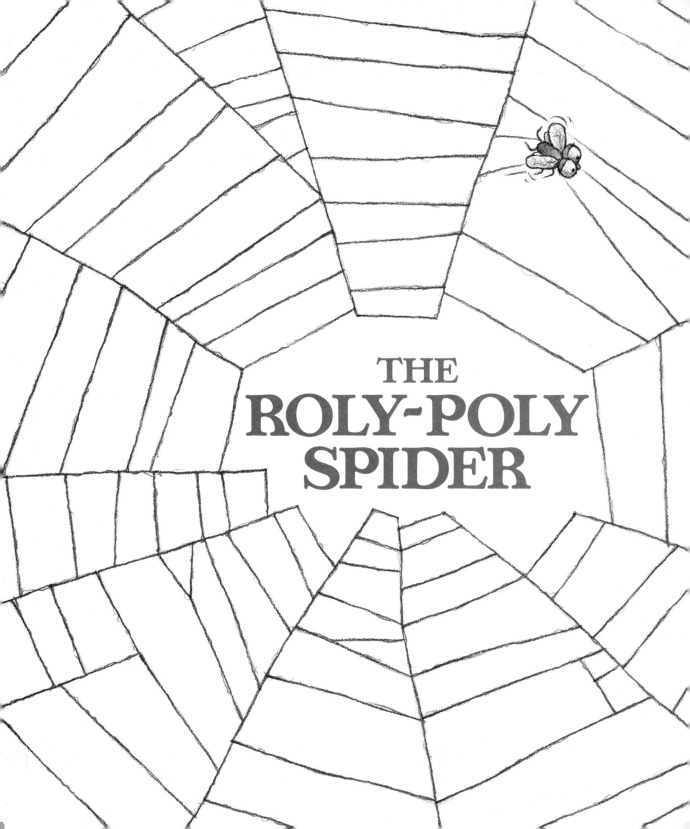

THE
ROLY-POLY
SPIDER

FIFTY EIGHT

THE ROLY-POLY SPIDER

by Jill Sardegna

Illustrated by Tedd Arnold

SCHOLASTIC INC.

New York Toronto London Auckland Sydney

With love to Heidi, Ross, and Jackie
—J.S.

For Ben and Leah
—T.A.

ISBN 0-590-47120-1

Text copyright © 1994 by Jill Sardegna.
Illustrations copyright © 1994 by Tedd Arnold.
All rights reserved. Published by Scholastic Inc.

12 11 10 9 8 7 6 5 4 3 2 1   8   5 6 7 8 9/9 0/0

Printed in the U.S.A.   23

Mr. Arnold used watercolor paints and colored pencils
to prepare the artwork for this book.

The roly-poly spider once spun a sticky web,

spun a sticky chair,
two couches and a bed.
"Come visit me," she cried,
"I'm as lonely as can be."

But the roly-poly spider was hungry, too —
you'll see.

The roly-poly spider was casting out a line;
she hooked a spotted beetle and reeled him in to dine.

"Sorry," said the beetle, "I really shouldn't stay."

But the roly-poly spider
drank beetle juice that day.

The roly-poly spider
spun on the garden lane.
She snagged a caterpillar
and asked him, "What's your name?"
He said, "My name is Lester.
I'm as handsome as can be."

Said the roly-poly spider,
"You look like lunch to me."

The roly-poly spider soon caught a bumblebee.
But he was fighting mad, so she waited patiently.
The more he fought, the more he stuck,
the more she smiled with glee.

And the roly-poly spider
had bee's knees with her tea.

The roly-poly spider set out a picnic treat.
Up jumped a ladybug, who stopped to talk and eat.
The time grew late; the treat was gone;
she wanted to be fed.

So the roly-poly spider
ate up her friend instead!

The roly-poly spider tossed out a silken thread.

Missed a skeeter's wing

and missed a sow bug's head.

At last her sticky noose roped in a great big fly.

Said the roly-poly spider,
"You'll be my shoofly pie."

The roly-poly spider was starving for romance.
Along came a millipede, who asked her for a dance.
"I'll teach you how to spin if you step into my web."

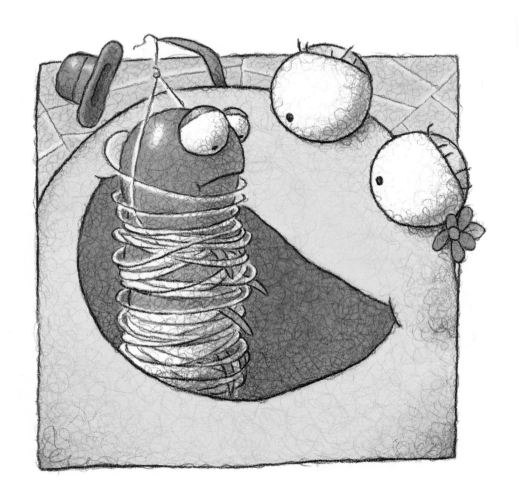

But the roly-poly spider spun him in her web instead.

The roly-poly spider went down a water spout.

But after all she ate, she was too fat to come out.
Stuck inside the middle, she was there to stay.

Said the roly-poly spider,
"I ate too much today."

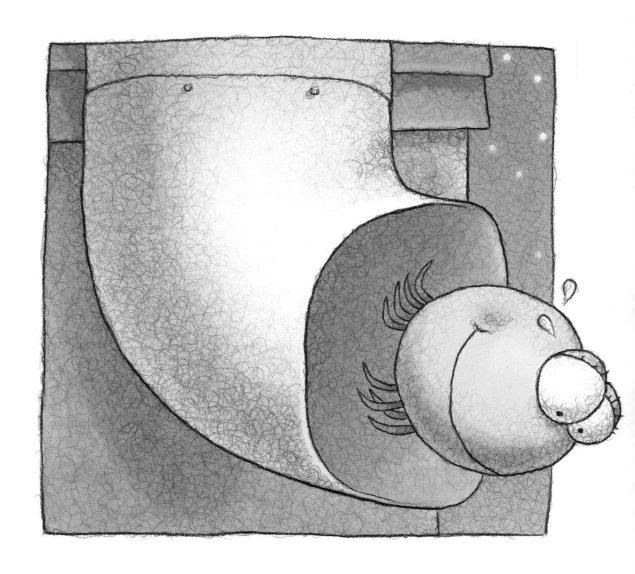

The roly-poly spider wriggled in the spout.
She wiggled and she wobbled till she finally popped out.

She looked up at the moon;
then she yawned and settled back.

Said the roly-poly spider,
"I need a bedtime snack!"